# Princess ✦ ✦ Stories ✦

## From Around the World

For Princess Dilly Daydream and Princess Chippie

with cuddles and kisses and love

*KT* (Mummy)


For Holly and Tess

*SW*

First published in Great Britain in 2004 by
Chrysalis Children's Books
An imprint of Chrysalis Books Group plc
The Chrysalis Building
Bramley Road
London W10 6SP
www.chrysalisbooks.co.uk
This edition distributed by Publishers Group West.

Text copyright © 2004 Kate Tym
Illustrations copyright © 2004 Sophy Williams

The moral right of the author and illustrator has been asserted

Designed by Sarah Goodwin and Keren-Orr Greenfeld

A CIP catalogue record for this book is available
from the British Library.

ISBN 1 84458 142 X

Printed in China

2 4 6 8 10 9 7 5 3 1

This book can be ordered direct from the publisher.
Please contact the Marketing Department. But try your bookshop first.

# Princess Stories

## From Around the World

*Retold by* Kate Tym

*Illustrated by*
Sophy Williams

CHRYSALIS CHILDREN'S BOOKS

# Contents

# The Frog Prince

*J*ust because someone doesn't look very nice on the outside doesn't mean that they're not rather lovely on the inside. Which is just what a certain little princess found out the hard way! Princess Pandora was a beautiful if somewhat spoiled young lady but, despite her material wealth, her parents (particularly the king) had also tried to instil in her the importance of being a good and honest person. However, sometimes the princess found it hard to live up to her father's expectations, and there was one such evening when her honesty was well and truly put to the test.

The princess had a favourite plaything–a golden ball that she loved to toss up in the air and watch tumble, sparkling, back down towards her. She was always thrilled when she managed to catch it again, and liked to test herself by throwing it higher and higher up into the air.

On this particular occasion, she got quite carried away with herself and threw the golden ball so high that when she stretched out her hands to catch it, it slipped right through her fingers and bounded away towards the deep spring that lay near the summerhouse in the palace grounds.

The princess was terribly upset. The ball was very precious and her father had warned her only that very morning to be careful with it. She peered over the edge of the grassy bank and into the deep, deep spring. Princess Pandora rolled up her sleeve and delved into the cool waters. It was no good: she couldn't even see the bottom and, being a princess, she wasn't enjoying lying on the muddy ground and getting her arm cold and wet. Instead, she decided, in true princess style, on the next best course of action, and promptly burst into tears.

Feeling the situation demanded one of her best performances, she let out a series of heart-wrenching sobs and gulped out her distress. "Oh, woe is me!" she sniffed, her pretty little nose going quite red at the end, as two tracks of tears threaded a path down each of her satin cheeks.

As she continued to lament her lost ball, a warty little head popped out of the water, followed by a warty little body, as a green slimy frog emerged from the spring and sat down beside her on the bank.

"Why are you crying?" the frog asked the princess, kindly.

"I've lost my golden ball," she wailed, her voice rising to a new pitch of distress.

"Oh," said the frog calmly. "Well, perhaps I can help you," he suggested.

The princess all but sneered, "Well, yes, obviously I would give a pile of precious things to anyone who could help me get my ball back. But you're … well, how can I put this? You're only a little frog– how can you possibly be of help to me?"

The frog didn't seem too put out by the princess's snub. "Don't you worry," he went on, "I'll get your ball back, but you must give me something in return."

The princess sniffed and blew her nose loudly in her lacy handkerchief.

Not to be put off, the frog went on regardless, "If I get your little golden ball back, you must do something in return. You must care for me and let me live with you. You must let me eat from your little golden plate and sleep upon your little bed. And for that, I will bring you your ball."

The princess didn't believe for one moment that her new friend would be able to fulfil his promise, but she decided to humor him, as she felt she had nothing to lose. "All right," she patted her eyes dry, "you have my word: fetch my ball to me and I shall treat you like a prince!"

The frog didn't hesitate for a second. With one almighty leap, he dived into the deep dark water of the spring and kicked his little legs behind him as he descended into the depths below. The princess waited, hardly daring to breathe. Before long, with a splash and a gasp, the frog broke through the surface of the water and jumped back onto the bank beside the princess, clutching in his webbed fingers the princess's beautiful golden ball!

"Here it is!" he announced, tossing the ball to the ground.

Well, the princess was so overjoyed she clean forgot her promise and leaped upon her treasure in delight, scooping it up and skipping off towards the palace without so much as a backward glance.

If she had looked back, she may have seen the frog standing on the bank with a disgruntled expression on his face. "Don't forget your promise," he called after her, but the princess was already almost out of view.

She ran and she ran all the way back to the palace and burst into the royal dining-room just in time to sit down to a wonderful ten-course dinner. But before the first morsel of the first course had touched her lips, there was a strange tap-tapping to be heard at the door.

The king looked up, startled. "Who on earth…?" he said in surprise, for he had looked over to the door and could see no one there.

"I'm down here," the frog said boldly, slipping through the door as a footman opened it.

The princess blushed—she'd never thought for a moment that the little fellow would be able to make it all the way from the spring to the palace. But surely her father would understand that she couldn't let a frog share her life? It really wasn't the done thing in royal circles, to have an amphibian to tea.

"What is it you want?" the king asked gruffly. He wasn't used to having his supper interrupted by creatures of any kind.

The frog explained the deal that had been struck between him and Princess Pandora. "I have merely come to claim my payment," he stated.

"Quite," the king said sternly. He turned to his daughter. "My dear," he said, "a promise is a promise. Now I suggest you help this little chap up to feed at your plate."

The princess was stunned. "But, Father!" she protested.

"Father nothing!" the king said firmly. "You made a promise, my dear, and I'm afraid you must keep it—no matter how distasteful you find it." He turned to the frog. "Er, no offense, old man."

The frog beamed back, hopping closer to the princess's chair. "None taken, Your Highness, none taken," he croaked.

So there was nothing for it, the princess had to share her meal with the persistent little frog and, as the day came to a close, she had to place him gently on her pillow that he might sleep through the night at her side.

In the morning, the princess sighed with relief as the frog leaped off her pillow and sprang off out through her patio doors. "Cheerio!" he called, as he hopped out of sight.

"Thank goodness for that!" she shuddered, remembering how his long pink tongue had flicked out to pluck a pea from her plate the evening before. "And good riddance," she said, shutting the patio doors tightly and vowing to stay safely in the palace for the rest of the day.

But that evening, events unfolded just as they had the day before and, at dinner-time, even before the hors d'oeuvres had touched the tablecloth, the little frog appeared, face pressed up against the French windows, begging to be let in.

Before the princess could protest, her father looked at her firmly. "Remember the example you set, my dear," he said. "A personage of such royal blood should never break their promise."

Princess Pandora felt suitably chastened, "Yes, Papa," she said meekly, and she walked over to the window and let the frog in herself.

Again, just as he had the night before, the frog enjoyed a sumptuous repast and then happily joined the princess as she made her way upstairs to bed. She'd more or less resigned herself to a lifetime spent in the frog's company and was not surprised when, once again, the next day's events unfolded in exactly the same way as before.

On that third night, she lay down with a heavy heart. *Whoever will marry me now*, she thought as she drifted into sleep, *knowing that they'll have to share their bridal bed with a frog?*

But as the sun's dappled rays ushered in the day the next morning, the princess was in for a surprise. Opening her bleary eyes and expecting to see her faithful frog at her side, she was greeted instead with the sight of a handsome prince gazing on her with the most dazzling blue eyes she had ever seen.

The princess didn't know where to put herself. It's not every day that you wake up with a dashing prince at the end of your bed.

"I... I..." she spluttered, completely lost for words.

"Fear not," said the prince, his voice like warm toffee, "it is I, Ferdinand!"

The princess still looked baffled as she clutched her bedsheet to her chest.

"The frog!" the prince declared. "I was under the spell of a malicious fairy who turned me into a frog. I would have stayed that way, too, if it hadn't been for you and your kindness in allowing me to share the very food you ate and the bed you slept in."

Pandora beamed. If she'd known this would be the end result, she'd never have left the frog by the spring in the first place! She blushed at the thought. But the prince was an understanding young man, aware that, given the circumstances, he may well have acted in the same way, and aware also that Pandora was far too pretty a princess to let slip through his (no longer webbed) fingers.

"My dear," he said. "Would you do me the great honor of becoming my wife and coming to live with me in my kingdom?" he asked.

And the princess didn't hesitate for a second before saying, "Oh, yes! Please!" (Because another thing the king had taught her was to always be polite.)

So remember, if you ever happen to come across a talking frog, with a green slimy skin and bulbous eyes, don't be fooled, for inside that warty exterior could beat a heart of pure princely gold!

# The Golden Touch

*T*his is a story that will make you think twice about being grasping or greedy. It involves a king who got his comeuppance for being just that. But don't let me spoil the story by telling you the ending before we've even begun. Let's start at the start, shall we?

Well, as I mentioned, this tale is about a greedy king. His name was Midas and he lived in a country called Macedonia. Now, Midas was a very wealthy man and he enjoyed all the trappings of his wealth. He lived in a fabulous palace filled with fantastic treasures and thought nothing more important than the pursuit of even more riches.

There was, in fact, only one thing in life that he loved more than money, and that was his daughter, the princess. She was a delightful little girl with not an ounce of her father's terrible money lust. She wouldn't have minded if she was poor as long as she had the things around her that made her happy— the sun, the air and a garden full of beautiful flowers.

Despite their different natures, Midas and his daughter did love each other very much and they loved spending time together walking through the splendid grounds that surrounded the royal palace. Midas often strolled around his garden on his own too, admiring all the wonderful things his great wealth had brought him and imagining the colonnades and temples he could build there if his wealth increased.

One such morning, he was walking along when he heard a snoring sound rising up from under a hedge. Midas was most put out—the palace grounds were private property—he didn't want some dirty peasant lying around under his hedge making the place look untidy. He stormed up to the hedge and gave it a good old shake. "Get out from under there, you unsightly wretch!" he ranted angrily, as a little hairy leg poked out from under the bottom branches. A smelly goat in his sculpted paradise! The king was furious and kicked out in the region of the goat's rear end. But, as the startled creature emerged from its resting place, it became clear that it wasn't a goat at all but a satyr: half-animal, half-man. And not only that, but it was a satyr that Midas knew quite well. His name was Silenus and he had a reputation for being the life and soul of any party.

It was clear from his bleary eyes and the empty wine flagons lying around him that Silenus had had quite a night! And in his befuddled state, the last thing he wanted to have to do was explain himself to mean old Midas. "Er... Sorry about the hedge..." Silenus stammered. "Bit of a heavy night..." he mumbled on, but Midas looked less than impressed. Time to try another tack, Silenus thought, forcing a look of contrition onto his face and squeezing a fat tear out of one eye. "Please forgive me," he wheedled, "I'm a foolish creature, I know I should be stronger, but I do so like a festive gathering... If you could only find it in your heart to forgive me..." he whined on.

But, before he could finish, his sentence was cut short by Midas's laughter. Midas was a greedy man but he wasn't without a sense of humor and he'd rather enjoyed Silenus's remorseful performance.

"On your feet, you old rogue," he chuckled, "what you need is a good breakfast—that'll soon have you feeling better." And, with a sigh of relief, Silenus followed the monarch to the palace for a feast fit for a king.

The king, of course, had very few friends, always worried that they were after his money, so it made quite a nice change for him to have a grateful guest to stay. So much so that he kept Silenus around for five whole days, listening to his stories and getting him drunk on velvety wine from the palace cellars. Silenus was having a high old time, but as the week drew to a close he began to worry that his master, Dionysus, lord of the satyrs, might be wondering where he'd gone.

So, Silenus returned briefly to the realm of the gods and told Dionysus of the kindness Midas had shown him. Dionysus was quite impressed with the generosity the greedy old king had shown his servant and decided to repay Midas with a gift.

Dionysus returned to Midas's palace with Silenus. They made their entrance in Midas's opulent throne room. "Midas," Dionysus boomed. "I hear you have treated my servant here with great charity, and in repayment I shall grant you any wish you care to name."

Although slightly taken aback at the sudden appearance of the deity, Midas didn't even need a second to think. Without a breath of hesitation he said, "My lord, grant that whatever I touch shall be turned to gold."

Dionysus granted his wish and quickly dragged the complaining Silenus away with him, only glancing back momentarily with a troubled look on his face. Midas was too caught up in his own cleverness to have any reservations over Dionysus's swift exit. He was over the moon—what a gift for one as grasping as him! He could hardly wait to put it to the test.

Midas skipped around the palace lightly touching everything in his path. Tables, chairs, drapes of rich cloth all turned instantly into solid gold. It was true! He had a golden touch! Soon the palace was awash in a golden haze and Midas sat in the middle of it in a golden hall, on a golden throne, grinning from ear to ear in the warm yellow light. Midas was in a fever of delight as he leaped down from his throne and headed out into his beautiful garden, wanting to work his magic there too. He touched the trees, the flowers and the very grass he walked on ... all turned instantly to cold hard gold.

Midas was beside himself with joy as he headed back to the palace for a celebratory meal–feeling sure everything would seem much tastier when eaten off a golden plate. He ordered up a hearty breakfast and sat contemplating how best to use his gift for the rest of the day. He was already sitting on a fortune (literally!) and with still so many things out there waiting to be touched, there could be no end to his ever-expanding wealth.

Breakfast arrived and Midas's smile widened as he reached for a freshly baked bread roll. What a wonderful life! But the smile soon dropped from his face as the soft bread turned to a hard cold lump halfway to his mouth. All the delectable morsels his servant had brought him met the same fate. Figs, peaches, grapes, all became nothing more than golden ornaments. The honey went from liquid to solid gold in the matter of a touch. Even the jug of milk mocked Midas with its solid undrinkable form.

Hunger nagged at Midas's stomach, but alongside hunger was another feeling–panic! Midas was beginning to realize that having a golden touch might well be more of a curse than a gift as he surveyed the feast of inedible baubles that lay before him.

A creeping chill trickled down his spine as his lovely daughter came rushing in from the garden. "Father," she wept, "something dreadful has happened. There is no birdsong, no beautiful colors and no wonderful scents from the roses any more. The garden is lifeless and barren. How can this be?"

The princess came towards him and fear clutched suddenly at Midas's heart. "Stop!" he cried, reaching out his hand in front of him. Cold dread filled his breast–one touch from him would seal his daughter's fate for ever. "Don't come any nearer, I beg you," he pleaded in panicked warning.

But the little princess was young and spirited, and after her distress in the garden she craved the reassuring touch of her father's hand. She rushed towards him just as Midas reached out his hand again and shouted, "Stop!" In chilling silence their fingers met and Midas's precious daughter stood frozen, a golden statue, arms outstretched towards her father, a tiny golden tear frozen on each of her perfect cheeks.

Midas wept inconsolably—he realized too late what a foolish and greedy man he was, and that through his greed he had lost the most precious thing he had ever had. No amount of gold could ever make up for the loss of his little girl. He remembered Dionysus hurriedly shuffling out of the palace and understood that the god may well have foreseen the dreadful fate that awaited him.

Sure enough, just as he had that thought, Dionysus appeared before him. "So, Midas," he said gravely, "didn't I grant you your very heart's desire? Are you not the richest man in the world?"

Midas sniffed miserably. "Yes, indeed I am, but I'm also the unhappiest. I have lost the most precious thing in the world to me, and without my daughter all these riches mean nothing. I beg of you, take away this golden touch and let everything be how it was before and I shall never again seek riches beyond the dreams of man."

Dionysus looked sternly at Midas. "Very well, but be sure you keep this promise."

"I will, I will," Midas sobbed, gazing at the lifeless statue of his daughter.

"Very well," Dionysus said. "You must go and wash in the waters of the River Paktolos. Let its waters flow over you and all will be as it was before."

Midas didn't waste a moment. He set off on his long journey straight away. It took Midas weeks to reach the river, as he was a shadow of his former self: misery and hunger had taken their toll on the king. But eventually he made it to his destination. Before letting himself be engulfed by the beckoning blue waters, Midas took one final test to remind himself of his folly. He reached up to pluck a juicy fig hanging from a nearby branch. He could almost imagine the taste of its soft flesh but, of course, the moment he touched it, the fig turned into a cold hard nugget of gold.

Midas sighed and eased himself into the soothing waters. He prayed Dionysus would be as good as his word as he let the river wash over him.

Back on the stony shore, Midas's fingers trembled as he reached out to pick a pebble from the beach. His breath caught in his throat as he half expected the gray stone to turn to gleaming yellow under his touch. But no, the speckled pebble remained as gray and plain as it had ever been and Midas felt he had never seen anything more beautiful in his life. Joy filled his heart once more and he could hardly endure the journey home for longing to see his daughter again.

And there she was, upon his return, running towards him across the lawn of their beautiful garden. It was with unspeakable joy that Midas took the little princess in his arms and felt the warmth of her skin against his.

All was as it had been before; the palace was back to its marble splendor and Midas could now enjoy the food and drink his servants brought him and was no longer weighed down with a robe of heavy gold. Only one small thing had changed, for his daughter—although as pretty and loving as before—was different in one little way. Her hair, once thick and dark, now had the appearance of the palest gold. That was clever old Dionysus's doing, to remind Midas of what happens when you let greed rule your world!

# The Kingdom Under the Sea

Sometimes, when we make a promise, we don't really know how difficult it might be to keep, or what the consequences might be if we fail to keep it. So it once was in Japan for a humble fisherman called Urashima Taro who didn't keep his word and who paid a tragic price.

Urashima was a kind-hearted fellow, hard-working, loyal and caring. He was respectful to his parents and gentle and kind to all living things. So, when he saw an upturned turtle lying stranded on the beach, it was only natural that he would pick the poor creature up and try to ease its distress. And as Urashima gently lifted the turtle into his arms, he stroked the sand from its flippers and cooed reassuringly as he carried it over towards the breaking waves.

Urashima then waded out into the water and placed the turtle carefully into its foaming embrace. "Off you go, venerable turtle," he called after the majestic creature, feeling relieved that the turtle would soon be safe back among its own kind, "and may you live for a thousand years!"

The next morning, Urashima set off in his little fishing boat, his baited line dragging lazily behind him. He loved to sail out beyond the rest of the little fleet, preferring the solitude of the deep ocean, where he could be alone in his small boat between the vastness of the sky and the cold depths of the sea.

And so it was that as he bobbed gently on the water he heard his name lapping against his boat, mingled with the sound of the waves. "Urashima! Urashima Taro!" a little voice beckoned him.

Urashima looked around him, convinced his ears must be playing tricks on him in the emptiness of the ocean. But as he looked around again, he saw a turtle paddling to keep pace beside his boat, and it seemed to be the source of the call.

"Is it you that calls me, venerable turtle?" Urashima asked the ancient creature.

"Yes, it is I," answered the turtle. "I am the daughter of the Dragon King under the Sea and yesterday you saved my life. So, in thanks, I would like to take you to Ryn Jin, the beautiful palace that exists deep beneath the waves."

Urashima was astonished. All those whose lives are connected with the sea have heard of the Dragon King under the Sea, and now here he was–talking to his daughter! He felt honored to accompany the turtle and lowered himself gently onto her back that she might carry him with her to her father's domain.

The turtle dived and dived, leaving the lapping waves of the surface far behind. Urashima held on tight and looked around him in fascination as they passed shoals of iridescent fish, flitting through forests of seaweed and corals. Mighty whales and ferocious sharks bowed in deference as the turtle-princess passed by and tiny silvery fish flitted playfully in her wake.

They dived and dived until Urashima felt that they could dive no more and then, suddenly, there before them was a sight so incredible Urashima felt he must surely be dreaming. There, on the very ocean bed, rose up a mighty palace, looming majestically behind a magnificent coral gate, its mother-of-pearl slates glinting in the gloomy light of the ocean's depths. As they approached the gates, the turtle drew to a halt and lowered Urashima gently to the ground. She then turned to a swordfish standing proudly on guard. "This is an honored guest from the land of Japan," she said. "Please escort him to the palace of my father." And with that, she flipped her flippers and disappeared into the murky water beyond.

The swordfish wasted no time in accompanying Urashima into a beautifully decorated courtyard, where a great company of fish awaited him and welcomed him to the palace before escorting him through its royal portals.

Upon entering the palace, the sight that greeted Urashima quite took his breath away, for standing before him was the most beautiful princess he had ever seen. She was dressed in a silken kimono shot through with threads of pure gold, and her pale face was framed by thick black hair that swayed gently with the motion of the water.

"Welcome to my father's kingdom," said the princess. "The land of everlasting youth, where summer never dies and sorrow never comes. May I ask you to stay here a while with us?" she asked gently.

Well, what could Urashima say? "My only wish would be that I might stay here for ever," he sighed wistfully, for never before had he felt the feeling of pure love that enveloped him when he gazed upon the beautiful princess.

"Shall I be your bride, then," the princess asked, "that we might live together always?"

Well, again, Urashima was quite overwhelmed. Could he really be so lucky? As he gazed into the princess's almond eyes he could think of nothing he'd like more than to spend each and every day of his life by her side.

And so it was agreed. The fisher lad and the Dragon King's daughter were to be wed and the Dragon King made sure they had a wedding celebration that would be talked about for years to come through all the waters of the world. There was a huge banquet with an array of entertainers: juggling octopuses, jousting swordfish and racing seahorses who flitted playfully among the assembled guests. And the princess looked breathtaking in a kimono that glittered like the scales of a thousand fish, and with a crown of starfish woven into her hair.

Once the celebrations were over, the princess took her new husband on a tour of the palace that would be his new home. Urashima marvelled at the beauty of his new surroundings and felt sure that he had made the best decision of his life. But one small thing nagged at his conscience: he had disappeared from the world of mortals without a single goodbye to the parents who had loved him and raised him from babyhood.

"I must go to my mother and father," he told his new bride, "and tell them what has become of me, for they must surely believe I have been drowned at sea and I must free them from such sorrow."

The princess seemed a little uncomfortable with Urashima's suggestion but, as it became clear his mind was made up, she agreed to help him fulfil his wish. "Then I must return to my turtle form and carry you to the land above the waves," she said. "But, before you leave, take this gift from me." And the princess gave Urashima a beautiful, three-tiered lacquered box, tied up with red silk cord.

"Keep this box with you always, but," she cautioned, "do not open it, whatever happens."

Naturally, Urashima gave her his promise, but of course, we all know how easily promises can be broken, too...

Once Urashima returned to the land of mortals he was overcome with a strange dread, for everything was not as it had once been. The land seemed strange and unfamiliar and he didn't recognize any of the people he passed along his way. And when he reached his parents' house, fear gripped more tightly at his heart. His childhood home was no longer there and a different dwelling stood in its place.

Urashima called out for his parents in panic. "Mother! Father!" he shouted, "What has become of you?" But when the door of the house opened, it was not his parents who emerged, but an old man whom Urashima did not know.

"Who are you?" Urashima Taro asked him. "What has become of my home?" And he explained who he was and how he had lived there all of his life.

The old man scratched his head. "I have heard speak of an Urashima Taro," he said quietly, "but his story is an ancient one... He drowned at sea, I believe, but that was hundreds of years ago and his parents are long dead."

Urashima staggered back in disbelief. He had only been gone a matter of days, how could his parents be so long dead? In a daze he retraced his steps back to the little beach where he had only just come ashore. He sank down onto the sands and held his head in his hands. "The land of everlasting youth..." he whispered to himself. "Three hundred years must be only three days in the kingdom under the sea."

And, as he sat, his fingers played idly with the red silk cord that fastened the lacquered box the princess had given him as a parting gift. Almost without thinking, he opened the first box. Three wisps of smoke came swirling out and curled their fingers around him; in the blink of an eye Urashima Taro turned from the sun-kissed fisherman of his youth to an old, old man with a wrinkled face and gnarled body. He opened the second box. There was a mirror inside it. He held it up and as he gazed upon the gray hair and furrowed brow of his reflection, his heart grew heavy with sorrow and regret.

Now he had nothing to lose, so he opened the third box. A crane's feather drifted out, brushed across his face and settled on his head. Instantly, the old man turned into a bird; an elegant crane that soared up to the heavens high above the heaving sea.

And as he soared upwards, he looked back down to the earth disappearing beneath his wings and saw, bobbing gently close to the shore, his beautiful princess-bride in her ancient turtle form. Their eyes met and a current of grief passed between them as their hearts burned with the pain of separation. And as the turtle-princess looked up at her beloved husband, she knew that he had been unable to keep his promise and that she alone must return to her father's kingdom far below in the depths of the cold dark sea.

# The Pigman
## and the Princess

Now, being a princess isn't necessarily a guarantee that you're going to be a nice person. Sometimes, good looks, royal blood and pots of money are a recipe for only one thing– a spoilt little madam. And sometimes, it takes a prince with a kind and humble nature to teach such a little miss a lesson.

One such prince was a very handsome fellow called Daniel who lived in a peaceful kingdom not particularly blessed with wealth. Although he was poor (by royal standards) the prince was a happy chap and valued the few things in life he did have.

The time came for the prince to take a wife and his thoughts started wandering to the pretty little princess in the neighboring kingdom. The princess's name was Mirabella and he decided that he should first entice her with thoughtful gifts. So, it seemed only natural to him that he should send her the two most precious things he owned.

He carefully packaged up his gifts and sent them off by messenger. "Be sure to treat them with the greatest care," he warned, for they were gifts that came straight from his heart.

The first thing he sent was a beautiful rose tree. It had grown on his father's grave and was of great sentimental value. It was also precious because it had rare and special properties: it bloomed only once every five years but, when it did, it was the most spectacular flower you had ever seen. Luckily for the princess, the timing was perfect and one heavy flower hung from the bush, emitting the most heady scent you could imagine.

The prince's other present was his pet nightingale. It too was a rare creature, sitting happily in its bamboo cage, singing all day long. And, not only that, but it could sing any melody in the world in perfect tune—quite a talent in a feathered friend, I think you'd agree.

Of course, the princess upon whom these gifts were being showered was used to receiving presents of a different kind— sparkling diamonds, opaque pearls and gowns of spun silk were more to her liking. But, nevertheless, a present is a present, and when these ones arrived Princess Mirabella couldn't help the feeling of excitement rising in her breast, for surely an engagement present must be even more grand than the usual golden carriages and jewel-encrusted crowns she got for birthdays, Christmases, and mid-week treats!

The prince's messengers bowed low as they presented the engagement gifts and awaited the princess's response. She pounced upon the packages and began ripping the wrappings off them.

"Oh," she said in disappointment as the beautiful rose bush emerged. Her pretty nose wrinkled in disgust, so ruined by years of sniffing expensive perfumes it was no longer able to appreciate the delicate scent of a single rose. "What is it?" Princess Mirabella snapped.

"Why, a beautiful silken rose," one of her maidservants put forward.

"Oh," the princess said, slightly heartened. After all, if it had been made just for her... She reached out and touched the bloom. "It's not a silken rose," she barked, "it's just something that's been pulled out of the prince's garden. Who does he think he is, sending me a pathetic plant? Is this his idea of a suitable gift for a princess?" But then she softened. "Oh, I see..." she smiled, "this gift is but a joke to show me he has a sense of humor and to make the real present seem all the more special!" Princess Mirabella smiled smugly at her cleverness and sauntered over to the second box.

As soon as the wrapping was removed, the beautiful nightingale began his magical singing.

"Oh, that's a bit more like it," the princess smiled, clapping her hands. "I do so like music boxes, although this one is a little plain..." She examined it more closely, hoping to wind it up and find a more interesting tune. "Hang on a minute," she snarled, banging the cage back down onto the table and shocking the nightingale into silence in mid-song. "This isn't a music box at all, it's a stupid garden bird! What on earth is this prince thinking of? Does he really think he can win my hand with such worthless junk? I'd sooner marry a pigman than someone as cheap as that!" she declared, stomping out of the room, her pretty cheeks flushed red in annoyance.

Well, the prince's messengers returned to the palace and gave the prince the bad news and, believe me, they didn't pull any punches in their description of Princess Mirabella's harsh response.

At first, Prince Daniel was sad. After all, it would have made life simpler if he could have found a lovely princess to marry straight away. But then he gave it some thought. "Well," he said to himself, "she may be pretty as a picture and rich beyond imagining, but manners cost nothing and she doesn't seem to have any. She may rather marry a pigman, but I'd sooner marry a pig!"

Feeling cheered, Prince Daniel decided to teach the spoiled little princess a lesson. He called for his oldest, plainest clothes (which wasn't a problem as all his clothes were fairly old and plain) and set out for the neighboring palace. On the way he found a muddy puddle, smeared his face with mud and, with his disguise in place, he got a job looking after the king's pigs.

He was perfectly happy in his new role. The pigs were friendly enough and he'd always enjoyed the outdoor life. And when the pigs were occupying themselves, he kept himself busy in another way. Unlike most princes who couldn't tell one end of a screwdriver from another, Prince Daniel had loved hanging around the palace workshops as a boy and had become quite a whizz at making all kinds of things!

So now he was more than capable of knocking up a thing or two and this time he turned his talents to making a little saucepan decorated with bells that played a simple tune. Not only that, but the time he'd seemingly wasted in pestering the court magician he now put to good use. You see, the saucepan was magical too: if you put your finger in the steam that rose up from it, you could smell what was being cooked in every house in the kingdom.

One day, the princess was walking in the garden when she heard the tinkling bells of the little saucepan. She was intrigued; why would there be music coming from somewhere as lowly as the pigsty? Against the wishes of her ladies-in-waiting, Princess Mirabella headed over to see where the tune was coming from.

She wrinkled her pretty nose against the smell of the pigs as she leant in to see what was what and came face to face with the muddy pigman-prince. The princess blushed, for despite his ragged appearance the pigman was very handsome and the princess was quite taken aback. "I... I..." she stammered. "Ask him how much he wants for that saucepan," she snapped at her maidservant, trying to mask her confusion in a show of annoyance.

"I shall accept ten kisses from the princess," said the pigman.

Princess Mirabella blushed even more—a right royal flush! As if a beautiful princess would stoop to kissing a lowly pigman, she thought indignantly. But he wouldn't change his mind, and besides, he was quite handsome... So, with her ladies-in-waiting crowding around her, the princess gave the pigman his ten kisses and quickly skipped away clutching her prize.

Prince Daniel wasn't finished with his little game yet, though. So, next time his pigs were happily rooting in the ground, he set to work making a little rattle that could play all manner of tunes. Then it was simply a case of sitting and waiting for the inevitable to happen. He was quite certain the nosy little princess simply wouldn't be able to keep away. And, sure enough, there she came, with extra ladies-in-waiting to hide her, just in case. And this time she faced an even greater demand: one hundred kisses and nothing less!

Well, despite being tutored by the finest teachers in the land, the little princess had a rebellious streak and she was quite enjoying her moments of naughtiness with the pigman in the pigsty. With a great show of chagrin she gathered her ladies around and proceeded to dish out her payment. Rather more enthusiastically than may be thought proper, might I add.

The king happened to be glancing out of the palace window at the time and was surprised at what he saw. "What on earth do we pay those ladies for? Certainly not to stand around gossiping by the pigsty!" he ranted and set off in his slippers to catch them unawares.

He crept quietly up behind them, waited until he was as close as could be and then bellowed at the top of his voice: "What's going on here?"

Well, you've never seen a group of ladies-in-waiting move so fast! They nearly jumped out of their skins, poor loves. And, as they sprang apart, the view confronting him gave the king quite a turn: his precious little peach of a princess was presenting the pigman with a string of kisses. And what's more, eyes shut and oblivious to the world, she carried on regardless!

The king rushed up to the canoodling pair and pulled them roughly apart. "Scoundrel!" he yelled. "Hussy! Remember who you are!" he reprimanded his sobbing daughter. "You're a princess, not a peasant! And as for you..." the king turned to the pigman-prince, "your punishment will come!"

Well, Princess Mirabella sobbed; the ladies shrieked and hollered and swooned; and the king stood crimson-faced—you could almost see the steam coming out of his ears. But throughout all the commotion, the pigman remained calm. He simply walked quietly over to the water pump, washed his face clean of mud and returned to the fray.

"How I wish I had married that prince who sent me the silly presents," Princess Mirabella moaned. "Then I'd be happily kissing him and none of this would have happened!"

"Well," the pigman declared, "you may be surprised to learn I am that very prince!" and he pulled out his certificate of princeliness as proof.

Well, the little princess blushed again—all this talk of kissing was making her head spin! But she did manage to flutter her eyelashes and pop a coy smile onto her face. After all, the pigman-prince was very good-looking and the princess wasn't too silly to realize when she might be on to a good thing.

"So you'd like to marry me after all, would you?" Prince Daniel smiled.

"Well... I..." the princess looked up at him from under her lashes and clasped her hands together in front of her in what she hoped was an attractive fashion.

"Well, I must admit it would be lovely–" Prince Daniel went on.

The princess was now puce with embarrassed delight.

"–if it weren't for one thing..."

The princess looked taken aback.

"I wouldn't marry you for all the tea in China," the prince finished abruptly. "You prefer the smell of a thousand cooking pots to the scent of one perfect rose, and the tinny jingle of a musical machine to the perfect song of a nightingale. You're not even fit to kiss a pigman, let alone be the wife of a prince."

And with that, he turned on his heel and left the king and princess with their jaws hanging open and the ladies-in-waiting standing in stunned silence at what they had just heard.

The princess was mortified, and made all her ladies swear to secrecy over what they had seen. But do you think she changed her ways? Of course not! She married the first pompous twit to pop the question and produced a whole brood of spoiled brats to drive her to distraction for the rest of her days.

And as for the prince? Well, he finally found a princess worthy of him; one who appreciated the finer things in life: not money and jewels and rich food, but flowers and music and true, true love. And what's more, they raised a family of ten penniless princes who delighted them daily. And, of course, they all lived very, very happily ever after.

# The Lemon Princess

Once, in the East, there lived a prince. He was a handsome fellow called Prince Omar. In fact, handsome hardly does him justice. He had a fine strong figure and deep brown eyes, and many a lady of the court went quite weak at the knees when Prince Omar walked by. So when it came time for him to take a wife, Prince Omar decided he was only going to consider someone with a rare beauty to match his own.

He searched and he searched, hoping to find the most beautiful woman in the kingdom to be his wife, but it was in vain. Of course, there were some very pretty girls around, but none had quite the perfect beauty Prince Omar so desired.

The poor prince was beginning to despair when an old lady of the court came to him with an interesting suggestion. "I know where you can find the princess of your dreams," she told the prince. "But you must follow my instructions carefully."

"Oh, I will," the prince declared. "If only you will tell me how I can find her."

"Well," the old lady went on, "the one you seek is three days' ride from here in a beautiful lemon grove surrounded by roses. Go there and you will find a lemon tree that bears three ripe fruit. Pick the lemons and carry them with you–but be warned–do not slice them open, no matter how great the temptation, until you are at a place where there is plenty of water. Do you see?" the old lady asked.

"Oh, yes," the prince said hurriedly, only half listening, as he dashed off to ready his horse for the long journey ahead.

The prince rode for three days and three nights and, sure enough, he came to a grove where the scent of roses hung thickly in the air. And there, drooping with the weight of its ripe fruit, was the tree he sought. Prince Omar carefully plucked the three lemons from their branches and placed them gently in his saddlebag, before setting off again back the way he had come.

Of course, it wasn't long before the prince's mind started to wonder at just what might happen if he were to slice the lemons open. How could he resist the temptation to find out what lay inside?

So he slipped from his horse, picked up one of the lemons and sliced it in two. Straight away, a beautiful girl rose up from the lemon—much more beautiful than any of the prospective brides he had seen so far. But the poor thing was in some distress, "Water!" she cried plaintively. "Please give me water!"

Unfortunately for her, the prince's kingdom was a desert land and water was rarely close by. So the prince could not fulfil her need and could only stand by helplessly as the beautiful girl simply vanished like a wisp of smoke in the wind, before his very eyes.

The prince was a little perturbed by this turn of events, but having a strong princely character he took this first setback on the chin, remounted his horse and continued on his way back to the palace.

Of course, before long he began to wonder if what had happened with the first lemon was simply a fluke … perhaps he should cut open a second lemon just to see.

Well, I expect you could easily guess what might happen, but the prince (although exceptionally good-looking) unfortunately didn't have your foresight. So, when he sliced open the second lemon, he still hadn't made sure he was within sight of a lake or a river or even a trickling stream. And when a second maiden even more beautiful than the first rose up and begged the prince for water, there was nothing he could do to help her.

"Oh dear," he said, the penny finally dropping as she melted away before him. "No more chances, I see—I must get to the river before I open my third lemon." And the prince rode on to the banks of a mighty river which cut his kingdom in two.

There he took the third lemon from his bag and held his breath as he pressed the blade of his knife into its firm flesh. Instantly a girl rose up from the fruit. She was even more beautiful than the previous two girls–her bright eyes sparkling, her skin smooth as a peach–and so beguiling that the prince was immediately smitten. "Water," she cried, "please give me water."

And, for once, the prince was prepared as, without ceremony, he plopped her straight into the river. Once immersed in the deep dark waters, she drank and drank with the thirst of a thousand years, until finally she was satisfied and emerged from the river with her black hair dripping sparkling droplets of water around her beautiful face.

The prince was stunned–never had he seen such beauty in all his life. And as the Lemon Princess smiled enchantingly at him, he felt his heart soar in his chest. "My love," he sighed, "you alone shall be my bride, my beautiful Lemon Princess." And he placed his cloak gently around her shoulders. "First though, I must fetch you some clothes to wear and a horse to ride on, for you should travel in comfort back to the palace. I hate to leave you, but fear I must."

"Don't worry," the princess reassured him, "I shall hide in this tall tree until you return." And she called out to the tree, which bent down and lifted her up into its topmost branches as the prince rode off into the distance.

Time passed and the Lemon Princess sat and waited patiently for her prince to return. She had a wonderful view over the river and the surrounding countryside, and soon saw a lowly servant girl coming along the road with a water jar she needed to fill at the river.

Unlike the princess, the servant girl had not been blessed with beauty. Her hair was a tangled nest and her skin was rough and parched. Yet as she bent down, she saw reflected in the water the face of the beautiful Lemon Princess, and in a moment of foolishness mistook it for her own.

"What a beauty I am!" she cried. "I always knew I was far too beautiful to be a servant!"

But her words soon stuck in her throat as she heard a sound from above, looked up, and realized her mistake as the Lemon Princess smiled radiantly down at her.

The servant girl found her voice. "What are you doing up there in that tall tree?" she asked with a pretence of kindness, for really the bitter taste of envy was already in her mouth.

"I'm waiting for my beloved prince to return," the princess replied. "We're going to be married and he has gone to fetch me fine clothes and a horse to ride."

Well, of course, jealousy rose further in the servant girl's breast, for she was just as harsh on the inside as she was on the outside. And she decided that she might gain something for herself from this acquaintance. "O, lovely lady," she called up, "why not let me come sit with you and help you pass the time?"

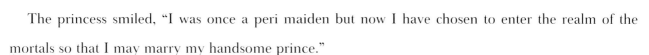

The Lemon Princess thought this a fine idea. After all, it was quite lonely sitting up in that tree all on her own and she had no reason to imagine that this passing stranger should in any way wish her harm. So the Lemon Princess got the tree to bend down and lift the servant girl up into its branches, too.

The servant girl wasn't sure what to make of this. "Tell me, O lady," she said, "are you human or one of the peri kind from the land of enchantment?"

The princess smiled, "I was once a peri maiden but now I have chosen to enter the realm of the mortals so that I may marry my handsome prince."

"Shall I comb your lovely hair?" the servant girl asked. She knew something of peri maidens and a terrible plan was forming in her mind.

"How kind you are," the princess sighed as the servant girl ran a comb through her beautiful thick hair.

"What might this be?" the servant girl asked, as she found a shining hairpin stuck deep in the princess's silky locks.

"It is my talisman," said the Lemon Princess. "Please do not touch it."

But, of course, her words were all the encouragement the servant girl needed and she pulled the pin sharply from the princess's hair. Well, as soon as she had, the princess changed into a white dove and fluttered frantically from the tree.

The servant girl laughed cruelly. Now all she had to do was sit tight and wait for the prince to come back. So she threw off her old clothes and let the river carry them away as she wrapped herself in the prince's cloak in preparation for his arrival.

When the prince arrived he couldn't believe his eyes—the beautiful princess he had left to wait for him was no more and in her place was a haggard-looking wretch. He tried his best to remain polite, but he was obviously rather shaken at the sight.

"My darling," he said gently, "what has become of you? Your skin, your eyes, your hair! They were so soft, so bright, so silken and now they… seem so changed…" he finished lamely.

"I know, my love. The elements have taken their toll as I waited for you, but fear not, time is a great healer, and when I am out of this baking sun and stinging wind, all shall be as it was."

Well, the prince had to take her at her word—what else could he do? For he was a man of honor and he had given her his promise. So he gently helped her into a silken robe and placed a necklace of delicately woven gold around her neck and bangles on her wrists, before helping her onto a snow-white mount and riding with her back to the palace.

Well, the people of the court really were in for a shock. The prince who couldn't find a woman beautiful enough to marry him had found a potential bride who was as ugly as any they had ever seen.

The king took his son to one side. "Are you quite sure of your choice?" he asked nervously, for he was slightly worried that after so much time riding through the desert his son had taken leave of his senses.

"I have given my word," the prince said. "And anyway, we shall not wed for forty days, by which time my Lemon Princess will be as beautiful as ever she was."

The king was not convinced, but felt he must let his son do what he felt was right.

If the truth were told, the prince was no longer sure of his choice either, and he spent much time walking in the palace gardens wondering over his decision. And it was on these walks that he heard the sad song of a white dove that came and sat upon the sandalwood tree.

The prince listened and was greatly moved by the music. "Is it not a touching lament?" he asked his servant-girl bride one day.

"Yes, my love," she replied, while in the very next breath she went to the gardener and commanded him to catch and kill the white dove and bury it deep in the ground. "It is Prince Omar's wish," she said, with breathtaking dishonesty.

The gardener did as he was instructed. But the next day, at the very place where the dove was buried, a great cypress tree sprang up, and when the wind sighed through its branches the sound was so sad as to make a tear well up in the eyes of anyone who passed by.

When the prince heard the sound of the wind in the cypress tree's branches he commented on it to his fiancée. "How sad a breeze blows by this tree," he said wistfully.

"Yes, my love," his intended replied quickly, trying hard to disguise her annoyance, before rushing back to the gardener and commanding him to cut down the tree and use the wood to make a cradle. "For the son I shall one day give Prince Omar," she said in false loyalty.

Well, the gardener once again followed his orders, cut down the tree and built a beautiful cradle for the future heir to the throne. But not all the wood was used and the gardener was a kindly man, so he thought to give the rest to the prince's old nurse for her fire.

The old nurse was most grateful and left the wood by the side of the hearth as she went out to do her shopping. As soon as she closed the door of her home, one of the sticks set to shivering all over and, before you could blink, it had turned into the most beautiful girl imaginable: none other than the lovely Lemon Princess herself.

The princess didn't waste a moment. She set to work making the nurse's home as clean and comfortable as it could be—sweeping the floor, washing the dishes and cooking a delicious meal that filled the house with the smell of warming food.

So when the nurse returned she was amazed, "Who can have done such a kindly thing?" she wondered out loud.

The Lemon Princess came forward at once. "It was I," she said. "And I wonder if you could do something for me in return?"

Well, of course, the old lady was delighted to help someone who had worked so hard for her.

"Please will you go to Prince Omar and tell him that in your house there lives a girl who can make the finest carpets in the kingdom, and if he will give you silk threads, she will make him the finest carpet ever seen."

It seemed such a simple request that the nurse thought nothing of going to the prince and returning with all the Lemon Princess needed to work on her beautiful rug.

Well, days came and days went, and before long forty days and nights had passed, and the day of the prince's wedding dawned bright and new. And as for the servant-girl princess, well, she was just as ugly as ever, with red-rimmed eyes and hair like a haystack and a heart as cold as stone.

But the prince felt duty bound to fulfil his promise. "I have given my word," he sighed in resignation.

So it was that he was a little distracted early that morning when his old nurse turned up with the carpet that had been painstakingly made for him. "Here is a wedding gift," she said, unrolling the carpet on the ground in front of the prince.

What a sight unfolded before them: an intricately woven rug in vivid colours, with the most beautiful scene played out in its threads! For there before him, just as it had been in reality, was the quiet little lemon grove with the scented roses around it, and in the very middle of the carpet a portrait of the most beautiful woman the prince had ever seen–the Lemon Princess!

"Who made this carpet?" the prince asked in astonishment.

"A girl who lives with me," the nurse answered, somewhat bewildered at the prince's urgent tone.

"Then bring her to me," he said.

So it was that the Lemon Princess appeared before the prince on the very day they were to be married.

"My darling, it is really you!" the prince cried, taking the Lemon Princess gently in his arms. "You alone are my beautiful Lemon Princess and you alone shall be my bride. But, tell me, where have you been all these long days?"

And the Lemon Princess wasted no time in telling her tale of deception and betrayal.

Well, the prince was furious and sent his guards to find the wicked servant girl. But news of the prince's rage reached her first and she took to her heels before the guards could reach her.

And what does it matter what happened to her? When, in the end, the most handsome of princes married the most beautiful of princesses and, in time, they had the most delightful of babies, too. Beautiful, gurgling babies that, when they leaned down to kiss them, smelled ever so faintly of lemon.

# Popocatepetl and the Princess

Sometimes, a story is sad enough to make you shed a tear but beautiful enough to make you hold it in your heart for ever—I hope you will agree that this is a story like that. Long ago in ancient Mexico, there lived a people known as the Aztecs. Theirs was an impressive civilization, and they built great cities, and constructed temples and palaces of breathtaking beauty. The Aztec capital was called Tenochtitlan and it stood where Mexico City stands today.

Now, the emperor of Tenochtitlan was a powerful man who lived in great splendor with his empress wife. They enjoyed many long years together, but it wasn't until they were advancing in age that they fulfilled the dream they held most dear and had a beautiful baby girl—the little princess Ixtlaccihuatl, or Ixtla for short.

The emperor and empress were doting parents and loved Ixtla with every fiber of their being. Their daughter was the most beautiful child, with satin skin, sparkling eyes and a smile that melted their hearts. With every year that passed, their pride in their daughter increased as they watched her grow into a beautiful and confident young woman. They could refuse their daughter nothing. Nothing, that is, until she became old enough to choose someone to share her life with…

Now the emperor became a very stern father indeed. You see, the weight of his position rested heavily on the emperor's shoulders. And as he looked ahead to the future, he saw that the responsibility for his empire would, in time, be passed on to his only heir: the princess Ixtla. He worried that if she married she would share the ruling of their precious empire with her new husband, and who could the emperor trust to take on such a role? He trusted no one but his beloved daughter and could not bear the thought of someone sharing his throne with her.

This caused Ixtla great pain. She had grown up surrounded by the brave warriors in her father's charge, and one young man had been her particular friend. His name was Popocatepetl, and he and the princess would meet whenever they could and go out of their way to cross each other's paths. What started with the occasional brief encounter, passing the time of day, grew into a deep and heartfelt friendship and, before the two of them could think how it had happened, they were very deeply in love and wanted nothing more than to marry.

"Perhaps if I talk to your father?" Popocatepetl suggested one day.

But Ixtla felt certain it would do no good. She herself had pleaded and pleaded to no avail. "But, Father," she had begged, "you know Popocatepetl—he's a loyal servant to you—how can you not trust him?"

But her father would hear nothing of it, and so the star-crossed lovers had to live their lives in unfulfilled longing, praying for the day when the emperor might change his mind.

As time passed, the emperor became an old man without the strength he had possessed as a youth. Encroaching old age made him vulnerable. His enemies, who lived in the surrounding mountains, realized the emperor's weakness and swarmed down to besiege the city.

It was a grave time for the emperor: not only was the city at stake, but the future of his family and the royal line were also at risk. If he lost his city and his power, then in turn, his daughter could never rule in his place. The emperor was sick with worry; he felt it his duty to lead his people, but his body was old and weak. Wary of appointing one man as leader, he devised a plan that he felt sure would bring out the best in all of his men. He offered the hand of his daughter in marriage to the warrior who was the bravest in battle and the most instrumental in foiling his enemies and lifting the siege. Such a warrior would have proved he was worthy of the emperor's trust.

The warriors were delighted—never had they had such an incentive to give their all. The poor princess, however, was not so happy. She felt betrayed and saddened to be the prize in such a contest and besides, she already knew who she wanted to marry! She loved Popocatepetl, and to be forced to marry anyone else would surely be more than she could endure.

As with all wars, it was a terrible and bloody affair that dragged on seemingly without end. Exhausted messengers returned to the city with news of how hard the men were fighting to save their home and claim Ixtla as their bride. Throughout the conflict, however, one man emerged to take the lead and fight more bravely than the rest. This warrior was none other than Popocatepetl! And it was he who led the final great charge that drove the enemy away from Tenochtitlan for ever. Imagine his joy at the realization that the love that had been denied him for so long was his to claim at last!

On the whole, the other warriors praised Popocatepetl, as he was truly an inspiration to them. But human nature being what it is, jealousy is never far away. And so it was with Popocatepetl. Some of the warriors could not rejoice with the rest, but held an envy in their hearts that made them wish ill upon the brave young man. They left the victory celebrations early and rode back to the city one night before the rest of their comrades.

The rogue warriors headed straight for the royal palace, keen to be the first to give the emperor the great news of the war's end. They told of the amazing scale of the final battle and spoke of great acts of daring and bravery. Then, finally, they added a piece of grave news that was completely without truth: they said that Popocatepetl was dead.

The emperor was shaken by the tidings. He knew that although Popocatepetl had died a hero's death, it would be no consolation to his daughter. And, as he had promised, she would now have to marry another. The emperor asked the warriors which of them had been the bravest in battle and who had led them to their valiant victory. The warriors looked very uncomfortable. Of course, they would never be able to agree on who they should put forward; after all, they would all like to marry the princess and become the next emperor themselves. So, they said nothing at all and the emperor had to wait for further news. In the meantime, though, he had the unhappy task of telling the princess about Popocatepetl. With heavy heart, he summoned his beloved wife and daughter.

The princess received the news in stunned silence. She turned away from her parents and went to her room. There she lay down and immediately became very ill. Ixtla was dying of a broken heart and there was nothing anyone could do to help her. If Popocatepetl was dead, the princess had no desire to live herself, and so she simply closed her eyes and let the last of her breaths slip gently from her body.

The next day, Popocatepetl and the victorious army returned to the city, triumphant. The people rejoiced as they processed through the city on their way to the palace. But the joy of Popocatepetl's triumph was soon to fade to grief.

The emperor greeted his men and heard how Popocatepetl had emerged as the natural leader and, as promised, would now like to claim the hand of his beloved. The emperor slumped down onto his throne and held his

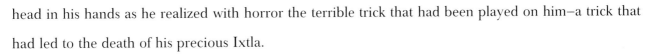

head in his hands as he realized with horror the terrible trick that had been played on him—a trick that had led to the death of his precious Ixtla.

"I have been a foolish and selfish old man," the emperor sobbed, as he told Popocatepetl of his daughter's passing. "I was too proud to let my daughter share my throne and now she is lost to me for ever."

Popocatapetl was grim with rage and grief. He sought out the jealous men who had brought false news of his death and, in his blind fury, he left not one of them alive. Then he returned to the palace, lifted Ixtla from her deathbed and gently carried her away. The people of the city followed him in a great procession. Although he walked for miles, he carried his love as steadily as if she were a sleeping child and the people followed as one, touched by the depth of Popocatepetl's sorrow.

Popocatepetl carried Ixtla's body far outside the city. They had often ridden there together in the low hills that surrounded Tenochtitlan. It was there they had felt freest and had been able to forget, if only for a short while, the terrible constraints on their love.

Popocatepetl gave a sign and the people rose as one, working together to build a huge pyramid of stones. They worked and worked until sunset, when they stood aside to let Popocatepetl climb alone to the summit, Ixtla still cradled in his arms. Once there, he gently placed her down and buried her under a heap of stones. And there he sat with her, through the darkness of night until the sun rose again the next day.

As daylight bathed the valley, Popocatepetl made his way back down the mound of stones and asked his warriors to prepare a second pyramid slightly higher than the first. And, when that was done, Popocatepetl climbed to the top and lit a torch of sweet-smelling resinous pine. He had no desire to claim his place as emperor, he only wanted to be close to his love and spend the rest of his life watching over her grave. And so he stood, holding a torch in memory of the princess who had died for the love of him.

The years went by and the seasons changed. Popocatepetl remained. Snows fell and the mounds of stone grew in stature till they were impressive white-capped mountains rising into the sky. Time passed and the beautiful city of Tenochtitlan fell to ruins, until eventually another city grew up in its place.

That other city is Mexico City and today it is overlooked by two beautiful snow-capped mountains named Ixtlaccihuatl and Popocatepetl, in memory of the lovers whose tombs they conceal. And from the mountain called Popocatepetl, a plume of white smoke still climbs. You can still see it, furling from the peak into the Mexican sky, a reminder of a lover's tragic vigil that never ever ends.

# Kate Crackernuts

Usually, princess stories are about princesses who are pretty as a picture and nice as pie. And this one's no different ... there is a pretty princess in it called Kate and, in usual fairytale style, she has a plain sister too. The thing is, the plain sister was called Kate as well! You see, the king had been married to a beautiful queen and they'd had a gorgeous baby girl whom they'd named Kate. But sadly, the queen died and the king decided to get married again. He managed to find a queen who was single (she was a widow too) and she also had a daughter (a plain one this time) and, by strange coincidence, she was also called Kate. Are you with me so far? So, anyway, in order to prevent years of confusion, the family decided that the pretty sister would be called Bonnie Kate and the less attractive sister would just be Kate.

Anyway, you know how it is in fairytales, generally stepsisters don't get along, especially if one of them's not so blessed in the looks department. But not this pair: they loved each other from the moment they met and got on like a house on fire.

Unfortunately, the perfect family set-up wasn't as perfect as it might first seem. The new queen was the mother of Kate-the-not-so-pretty. And the fact that her daughter wasn't the looker of the family made her really mad. The more time that passed, the madder she got. In the end she was so furious that she decided to do something about it. She decided to "ugly-up" Bonnie Kate to such a degree that her Kate would be a real catch by comparison.

Fortunately for the scheming old queen, she had a couple of good contacts in the field of spell-casting and she went to have a chat with one of them. The person in question was a miserable old witch who kept a flock of hens not far from the castle gates. Together she and the queen hatched a plan.

"Send the lassie to me," said the hen-wife, "without a bite to eat or a drop to drink, and I'll fix it so she's not so pretty any more."

The next morning, the queen put her plan into action. She sent Bonnie Kate off to fetch a basket of eggs, expecting her to come back with as ugly a mug as was possible to imagine. But she hadn't banked on the little princess's healthy appetite. On her way out of the castle she'd popped into the kitchen and spotted a plate of oatcakes. Well, who could resist? Certainly not Bonnie Kate, who was particularly partial to an oaty nibble of a morning. So off she went, with her pretty face stuffed full of oatcake and a happy spring in her step.

She got to the hen-wife's hovel and picked up the eggs for breakfast. The hen-wife called her over to the stove. "Lift up the lid on this pot," she said, "and see what you can see."

Bonnie Kate lifted the lid and a cloud of steam rose up, leaving a drop of water glistening on the end of her pretty nose and nothing more. The hen-wife was positively put out. "Go home and tell the queen to keep her larder locked in future!" she snapped. Bonnie Kate had no idea what the old crone was wittering on about, so she smiled politely and headed for home.

The next morning, the queen, who was not used to not getting her own way, sent Bonnie Kate off again on her egg-collecting mission. First stop, Bonnie Kate thought, the kitchen (for a little something to help her on her way). But she was disappointed; there wasn't an oatcake in sight and someone had even put a new lock on the larder door! Still, the thought of a nice fried-egg sandwich on her return spurred her on her way. Now, Bonnie Kate liked a chat so when she saw an old man picking peas, she stopped to pass the time of day. And the old chap was so delighted to have spent time with such a polite young person that he shared his peas with her. And very delicious they were too.

Back at the hen-wife's hovel, it was a repeat of the day before and, once again, when Kate lifted the lid off the witch's pot, nothing but steam engulfed her. Kate had no idea why she was to keep checking a pot of boiling water and she was beginning to wonder if the old woman wasn't completely losing her marbles!

And, added to that, the hen-wife seemed extremely miffed for no apparent reason. She virtually pushed Bonnie Kate out of the door snarling, "Go home and tell the queen if she wants something done, she must come herself!"

So, the next morning, the queen (who was, by now, puce with rage) decided to accompany Bonnie Kate herself on her journey. Bonnie Kate couldn't really see why there was so much fuss being made over half a dozen eggs but, if the queen wanted to waste her morning, who was she to argue?

Back at the witch's hovel, it was the same old story. "Lift the lid on the pot and see what you can see," she wheedled.

Bonnie Kate lifted the lid and this time, with a resounding squelch, a sheep's head rose up out of the pot and jumped onto her shoulders. In a matter of seconds she went from being Bonnie Kate to being Sheep's-head Kate and, believe me, it was not a pretty sight!

The queen, of course, was delighted–her own Kate was definitely the prettiest now! (Admittedly, there was not much of a contest when the only competition was a grass-munching ewe, but the queen was much too jealous to worry about that.)

Now, the queen's own daughter, not-so-pretty Kate, didn't share her mother's ambition for her to be glamorous princess material and she was absolutely horrified when she saw the state her poor sister was in. She knew that as long as her mother ruled the roost, the kingdom would not be safe for now-not-so-Bonnie Kate, and that she had better get them both out of there, and fast, or who knew what her mother might do next!

So off they went, with Bonnie Kate swaddled up in a blanket so as not to scare the unsuspecting public. They walked and they walked and they walked, until finally they made it to another kingdom. But Kate knew that if they were going to survive on their own she would have to work for a living, so she went to the only place she knew anything about—the local palace—and got herself a job as a kitchen maid. Luckily for her, there were added perks: a room in the attic and enough food to keep her and her woolly sister well fed.

As it turned out, the king of this kingdom was in a similar predicament to the two Kates. He had two sons and one of them was somewhat under the weather. All day, every day, the poorly prince lay in his bed fast asleep and not a soul could rouse him. And not only that, anyone who sat watching over him of a night-time disappeared and was never seen again. Well, obviously, after a while no one wanted the job of night-watch person at the prince's bedside. The king simply couldn't find anybody brave enough for the job. But then, of course, he hadn't counted on the incredible courage of kitchen-maid Kate.

Kate mulled over the vacancy and decided she'd give it a go—at a price, of course! "I'll do it for a bag full of silver," she said. And the king quickly agreed.

So, that night, Kate sat by the bedside of the sleeping prince. It was a pretty boring job as he didn't move an inch. Kate was on the brink of nodding off herself when the palace clock struck twelve. All of a sudden, the prince sat up in bed, swung his feet to the floor and stood up. In a complete daze, he dressed himself and headed out of the door. Now a lot of people may have been scared to follow, but not our Kate! She was up and after him like a shot. And when he headed to the stables and leaped onto his horse, she jumped straight up there after him as he set off into the night.

It was a strange journey to be making in the dead of night, with the prince's dog trotting along beside them, but Kate was always up for an adventure and, as they wound through some hazel woods, Kate picked some hazelnuts from the branches and stuffed them into her apron pockets. You never know in fairytales just when something might come in handy.

On they rode, until they came to a green hill where the prince called out,

"With his horse and hound at the end of his ride,

Open, open, green hill and let the prince inside!"

"And," Kate added, thinking quickly,

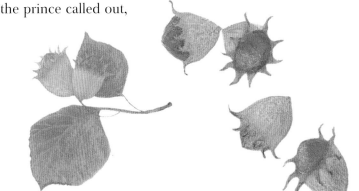

"Hide not the entrance, close not the gate,

Till safe inside is his fair lady Kate!"

Well, she thought, in for a penny, in for a pound.

A door opened in the hillside and they passed through it and into an incredible ballroom. Kate could hardly believe her eyes. The room was aglow with the light of a hundred sparkling chandeliers and rich velvet drapes hung on the walls. Kate stood mesmerized as she watched the most beautiful people she had ever seen whirling around the floor as they danced to the catchiest music she had ever heard.

Before anyone could spot her, Kate quickly slipped into the shadows out of view and hid quietly. The prince, meanwhile, was having a grand old time, surrounded by beautiful ladies who danced with him each in turn. He danced and danced and never stopped. No wonder he had to spend all day in bed!

Despite appearances, Kate realized that this was no life for the prince. She knew that his dancing partners were fairy folk, and that the prince had fallen under their spell, losing his free will. She also knew that she herself was in danger, for if they spotted her she'd be next on the long list of prince-minders who had disappeared in the night.

Soon, Kate noticed a fairy child playing with a silver wand. "You watch what you're doing with that," one of the fairy folk said to the girl. "Three strokes from that wand and the sheep-headed princess would be right as rain again!"

How lucky was that? Kate could hardly believe it. She gathered her thoughts, pulled a handful of hazelnuts from her apron pocket and rolled them towards the fairy child, one at a time. She rolled them and rolled them until the child dropped the wand and ran off to chase after the nuts.

*Gotcha!* Kate thought to herself as she tiptoed over to claim her prize.

As dawn broke and a cock crowed to announce the morning, the prince re-mounted his horse and Kate quickly leaped up out of the shadows and settled herself behind him as he headed back to the palace and his warm cosy bed.

Once he was safely tucked in, Kate sat by the fire cracking nuts and contemplating the events of the night before. She decided that it might be best if she kept what she knew to herself. So when the king and queen and the prince's younger brother came to check on them in the morning, Kate reported that the prince had had a good night and that was all.

Still, the king was impressed. Kate was the first person to make it through the night at the prince's bedside so he asked her if she'd like to take a turn for a second night running.

"Sure," Kate said, "but this time I'll have a bag full of gold, please." She knew how to drive a hard bargain, that girl.

So Kate had another night of prince-watching to look forward to, but before that there was something very important she had to do. She rushed up to the attic room to find her sister. There sat Bonnie Kate looking as sheepish as ever. Kate didn't waste a second–she whipped out the silver wand and touched her sister with it three times. And, hey presto! The sheep's head vanished and, to the delight of both princesses, her sister appeared looking just as gorgeous as she had been before.

That night, Kate resumed her seat by the prince's bedside. Everything happened exactly as it had the previous night. The clock struck twelve, the prince arose, dressed and headed out of the door. He mounted his horse and Kate leaped up behind. They set off on the same route and again Kate picked some hazelnuts on the way–well, they had come in handy the night before!

Once more, they came to the green hill and the prince called out,

"With his horse and hound at the end of his ride,

Open, open, green hill and let the prince inside!"

And again Kate chipped in,

"Hide not the entrance, close not the gate,

Till safe inside is his fair lady Kate!"

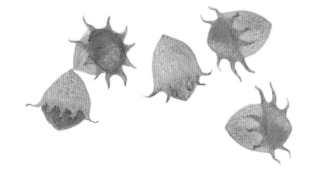

In they went and off the prince pranced for a night of partying with the fairy folk.

Kate faded into the shadows once again. She watched carefully and noticed a fairy child chasing a white bird. One of the fairy folk came over and spoke to the boy. "You be careful now, for if anyone roasted that bird, just three mouthfuls would set the prince free from our enchantment and make him as well as ever he was."

What a piece of information! Kate simply had to get her hands on that bird. So, she took some hazelnuts out of her apron pocket and started rolling them towards the child. Well, what child can resist a game of marbles? The fairy child left his game with the bird and headed off after the nuts. Quick as a flash, Kate snatched up the white bird and hid it under her apron. She then waited patiently for the cock to crow so she could make her escape with the prince.

Back at the palace with the prince once more tucked up bed, Kate swiftly killed the bird, plucked off its feathers and put it on a spit over the fire. Soon the smell of roasting bird drifted over to the sleeping prince. His nose twitched and he opened his eyes.

"Something smells good," he said sleepily.

"Here, try this," Kate said, offering him a bite of bird.

"Mmm, delicious," he said, raising himself up on one elbow.

"Have another mouthful," Kate encouraged him.

"Fantastic," the prince mumbled with his mouth full.

"Just one more bite," Kate smiled as the prince stuffed the third forkful into his mouth.

Well, you've never seen anything like it! He leaped up from his bed and sat down at the fireside next to Kate as if nothing had ever been any different. And there they sat until morning, cracking nuts and chatting like old friends.

When the prince's family came in to check on him, they could hardly believe their eyes. The king was absolutely over the moon. "I'll tell you what," he said. "I know I promised you a bag full of silver and one of gold, and I'll keep my promise too. But that was just for watching over my son, and now you've cured him too! That's worth more than any money in the world. What else can I give you? Is there anything you would like?"

Kate didn't even have to give it a moment's thought. Having spent the last couple of evenings with the prince and the whole morning chatting, she'd taken quite a shine to him. "What I'd like best," she said boldly, "is to marry the prince!"

The king was delighted, as was the queen; they quite liked the idea of having a feisty kitchen maid for a daughter-in-law. And the prince was thrilled to bits. That morning had been the best he'd had in years and he couldn't wait to spend more time with his new love.

Not only that, but on meeting Kate's pretty sister, the prince's younger brother thought he'd make it a matching set and marry Bonnie Kate, too. So a double wedding was arranged, with the two princes marrying the two Kates.

So there it was again, two Kates in the same family. And, after her experience with the sheep's head, Bonnie Kate didn't really fancy being called "Bonnie" any more. Instead, to save confusion, the prince who'd been ill gave a new name to his wonderful clever Kate. He called her Kate Crackernuts because it was when they were sitting by the fire together, cracking hazelnuts, that he'd first come to love her.

Ahhhh! Now that's what I call a fairytale ending!